בס"ד

This book belongs to: לה׳ הארץ ומלואה

Please read it to me!

PEANUT BUTTER & JELLY FOR SHABBOS

BY **DINA ROSENFELD**

ILLUSTRATED BY
NORMAN NODEL

Hachai
PUBLISHING

Dedicated to our beloved children
Rivkah Malca,
Daniella Esther,
Meir
and Rayzel

Pamela and George Rohr

Peanut Butter and Jelly for Shabbos

For my children - May you always have the courage to try. *D.R.*
In memory of my dear wife Helen. *N.N.*

First Edition - Kislev 5756 / December 1995
Sixth Impression – Shevat 5767 / February 2007

ISBN 13: 978- 0-922613-69-4
ISBN 10: 0-922613-69-9

LCCN: 95-75435

Hachai Publishing
Brooklyn, New York
Tel: 718-633-0100   Fax: 718-633-0103
www.hachai.com — info@hachai.com

Printed in China

• •

Modeh Ani – morning prayer   **Tzedakah** – charity
Shabbos – Sabbath   **Davened** - prayed

PEANUT BUTTER & JELLY FOR SHABBOS

Yossi opened his eyes one cold winter day
Then said 'Modeh Ani' and washed right away.
"This Friday is special," thought Yossi, "because...
There's a reason..." But he just forgot what it was!

Then Father walked in and called, "Hey, sleepyheads!
It's time to get up; jump out of your beds.
You're mother's been gone for three days, and we've missed her;
Today she comes home with your new baby sister!

"I'll pick up your grandmother; she'll help us, too.
Since Shabbos starts early, there's so much to do!
Stay with your grandfather; I'll be back soon –
Please polish your shoes and clean up your room!"

So the boys gave tzedakah; they davened and ate
They wiped off the table, and each washed his plate.
They cleaned up their room, gave their shoes a good shine,
And for Mother they colored a 'Welcome Home' sign.

"Hey, Laibel," asked Yossi, "what's taking so long?
When are they coming? I hope nothing's wrong!"

"Look outside!" pointed Laibel. "The cars are so slow.
The road must be icy – it's starting to snow!"

Laibel and Yossi could hear the wind blow
As their yard disappeared under layers of snow.
With cold noses pressed to the glass, they sat there
Watching the snowflakes whiz by through the air.
Their eyes opened wide; they smiled in delight
And their breath made the window all frosty and white.

"Let's go out," Laibel said. "It's sticking just right,
And I'm in the mood for a big snowball fight!"

Yossi smiled and then frowned with a shake of his head.
"But Laibel, we have work to do here instead."

"It seems everybody is coming home late.
Who will make food for Shabbos? We simply can't wait!"

"We're in trouble," said Laibel, "if we touch a knife,
And we never made Shabbos ourselves in our life!
If we turn on the oven, I know we'll regret it.
Cooking's too hard, so I say let's forget it."

"We can't give up now," was his brother's reply.
We'll only succeed if we're willing to try!"

They sat for a minute; they sat there for two
Until Yossi came up with one thing he could do.
"I can't cook gefilte fish, that may be true,
But I always make tuna – and that's a fish, too!"

"I can't touch a knife," Laibel said, "that I know,
I can use a peeler for cucumbers, though."
So the two boys washed up with soap in the sink
And both started working before you could blink.

"Soup's a problem," said Yossi, "so this afternoon
I'll prepare something else we can eat with a spoon."
He took down the bowls with the fancy gold rim
And filled them with applesauce, up to the brim!

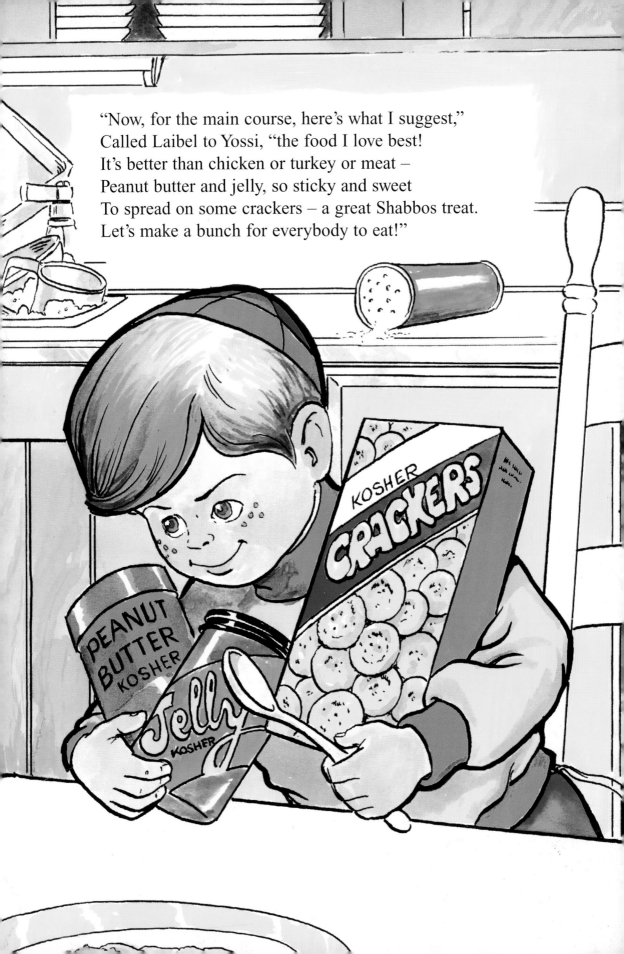

"Now, for the main course, here's what I suggest,"
Called Laibel to Yossi, "the food I love best!
It's better than chicken or turkey or meat –
Peanut butter and jelly, so sticky and sweet
To spread on some crackers – a great Shabbos treat.
Let's make a bunch for everybody to eat!"

Soon the meal was ready, but Yossi cried, "Laibel –
We haven't got challah on our Shabbos table!"

"Don't worry," said Laibel to Yossi, "don't cry –
We'll only succeed if we're willing to try."
Waving two frozen bagels over his head,
Laibel grinned. "Don't you see? We'll use bagels instead!"

"Now for Shabbos dessert," Yossi said, "there's no cake.
Isn't there anything else we could make?"
"We don't need it," said Laibel. "We made so much stuff!
Just look at the table; I think that's enough."

"Wait a minute!" said Yossi. "Won't this do the trick?"
And he pulled from his pocket a red candy stick!
He broke it in bits which he put on a plate,
And Laibel said, "Yossi, that candy looks great!
Sometimes you're really a pretty smart guy –
But you'll only succeed if you're willing to try!"

Just then came a knock and a key in the lock;
In walked the family – and oh, what a shock!

Grandma's right hand held a big covered dish
That she'd filled with her homemade gefilte fish.
Her left hand held platters of kugel and cake
And fresh challah, as only a grandma can bake.

Father carried in matzoh ball soup, piping hot
And roast chicken and meat in a huge, steaming pot.

Mother carried a bundle in her arms, too–
Their own baby sister, so tiny and new!

"Mazel tov," Mother said, "for your new baby sister!"
Then Yossi and Laibel ran over and kissed her.

"We knew," said the boys, "there'd be no time to cook,
So we made the whole Shabbos ourselves. Come and look!"

"It was fun," Laibel added, "as easy as pie.
We succeeded because we were willing to try!"

Shabbos Table

We Love Bab

We love

Grand

Then Father took pictures of Yossi and Laibel
Standing right next to their own Shabbos table!

That night, they ate tuna and gefilte fish,
Then applesauce and soup for the second dish.
Next came cucumbers, kugel, roast chicken, and meat,
With peanut butter and jelly, so sticky and sweet.

For **dessert**, there was cake and the red candy stick,
Whi**ch** they finished right down to the very last lick.

They looked at the baby and touched her soft skin.
They patted her fingers and tickled her chin.
Yossi said, "She's the best baby I've ever seen."
"Pretty cute," said Laibel, "for a girl, I mean.
When she's bigger, we'll teach her – Yossi and I –
That you only succeed if you're willing to try!"